T

....

with love

From...

To my parents.
Britta

LITTLE TIGER KIDS

(an imprint of LITTLE TIGER PRESS)

1 The Coda Centre, 189 Munster Road, London SW6 6AW

www.littletiger.co.uk • First published in Great Britain 2014

Illustrations copyright © Britta Teckentrup 2014

All rights reserved • ISBN: 978-1-84895-886-9

Printed in China • LTK/1800/0108/0514

2 4 6 8 10 9 7 5 3 1

The Twelve Days of
Christmas

Illustrated by
Britta Teckentrup

On the **first** day of Christmas,
my true love gave to me…

a
partridge
in a
pear tree.

On the **second** day of Christmas, my true love gave to me...

2 turtle doves

and a partridge in a pear tree.

On the **third** day of Christmas,
my true love gave to me…

3 French hens, 2 turtle doves,
and a partridge in a pear tree.

On the **fourth** day of Christmas,
my true love gave to me…

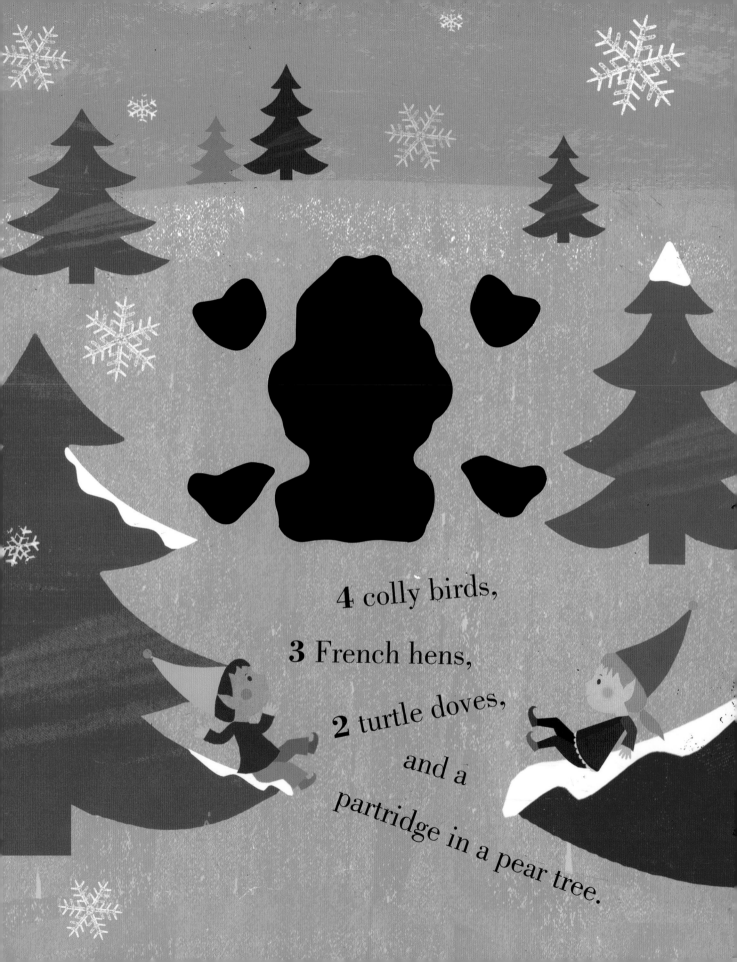

4 colly birds,

3 French hens,

2 turtle doves,

and a

partridge in a pear tree.

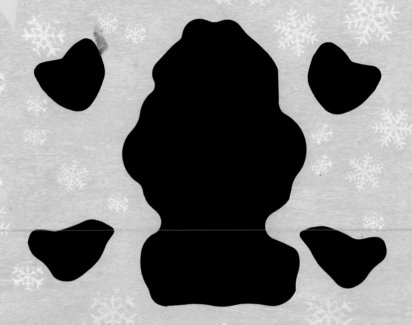

$\mathbf{O}$n the **fifth** day of Christmas,
my true love gave to me…

5 gold rings,
4 colly birds,
3 French hens,
2 turtle doves, and a
partridge in a pear tree.

O n the **sixth** day of Christmas,
my true love gave to me...

6 geese
a-laying,

5 gold rings,
4 colly birds,
3 French hens, **2** turtle doves,
and a partridge in a pear tree.

On the **seventh** day of Christmas,
my true love gave to me…

7 swans a-swimming,
6 geese a-laying, 5 gold rings,
4 colly birds, 3 French hens, 2 turtle doves,
and a partridge in a pear tree.

On the **eighth** day of Christmas,
my true love gave to me…

8 maids a-milking, **7** swans a-swimming,
6 geese a-laying, **5** gold rings,
4 colly birds, **3** French hens,
2 turtle doves, and a partridge in a pear tree.

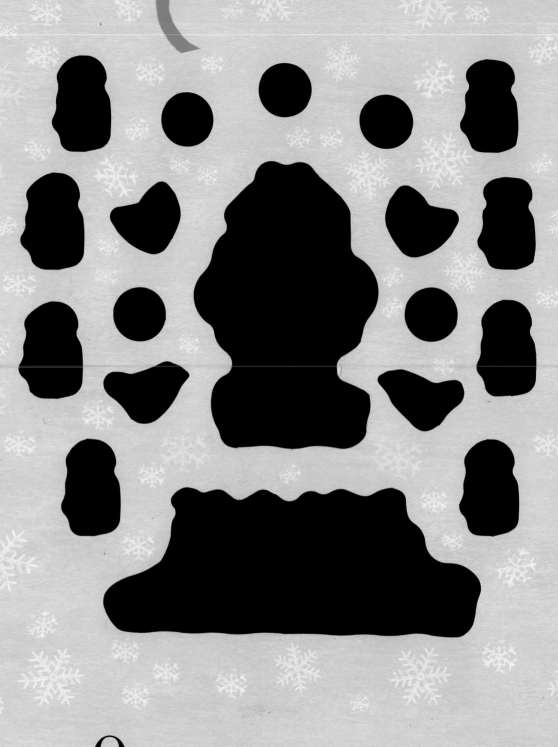

O n the **ninth** day of Christmas,
my true love gave to me…

9 ladies dancing,

8 maids a-milking, **7** swans a-swimming, **6** geese a-laying, **5** gold rings, **4** colly birds, **3** French hens, **2** turtle doves, and a partridge in a pear tree.

On the **tenth** day of Christmas,
my true love gave to me…

10 lords a-leaping, **9** ladies dancing, **8** maids a-milking,
7 swans a-swimming, **6** geese a-laying, **5** gold rings, **4** colly birds,
3 French hens, **2** turtle doves, and a partridge in a pear tree.

On the **eleventh** day of Christmas,
my true love gave to me…

11 pipers piping, 10 lords a-leaping, 9 ladies dancing,
8 maids a-milking, 7 swans a-swimming, 6 geese a-laying,
5 gold rings, 4 colly birds, 3 French hens, 2 turtle doves,
and a partridge in a pear tree.

On the **twelfth** day of Christmas,
my true love gave to me…